Easter Canticles

ADELE SERONDE

EASTER CANTICLES

ISBN: 987-0-578-50325-7
Pegasus Publishing

Published by Adele Seronde
Sedona, Arizona

Covers: Adele Seronde

Please accept these few hopeful wishes for this
time of loving. It is a moment for reaching out
to each other, for admiring the living creatures
of the Earth, animals, birds, plants, insects, even
the rocks and waters and sky.

It is our time to rededicate ourselves to protecting
and nurturing each other and our Earth itself. It is
a season for turning money and power into energy
of love, for using all our natural energies to create
newly charged lives, exciting experiments and
lasting solutions.

Even for short moments and short lives, flowers
give such fragrance, color and beauty, they unite
the whole world.

Be as flowers!

Songs of new springs
of longing
fill my heart.
I am of all birds
the dove.

I become rich waters
running wild
into new aquifers
of love.

We are alive now
        in glowing splendor
God grows in strange beauty
            above
        opening earth:
new anenomies
iris and gray pussy willows
            that move.

Shall we know strong fragrances
in transformed air?
Radiance
of God's breath?

Fire is upon us!
    Suns of whole universes heat
        our souls
    to faith.

How are we moving?
Lithe as leaping deer
        prowling as wilderness wolves?
Do we echo the dolphin's dive
        or the whale's deep plunge?
Yes, we are dancing
breath of wild creatures in love.
        Mating season of elephants
                to health.

Now is the time of resurgence
when things come alive
in joy's strong health.

Where is transformation?
All around us!
In buds become flowered
hope.

Dear Lord, thank Your grace
of your nurture,
of food for all mankind,
of love.

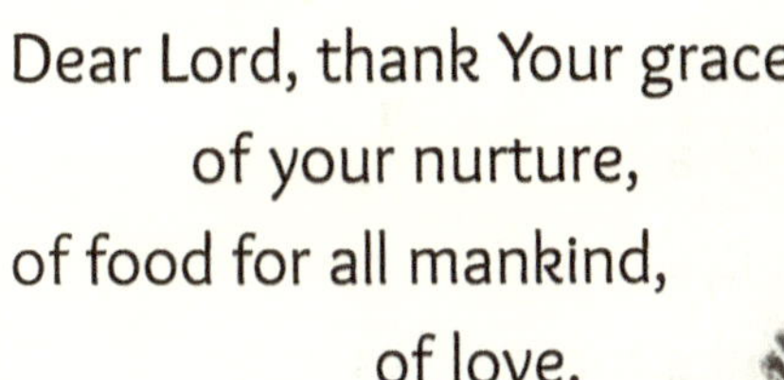

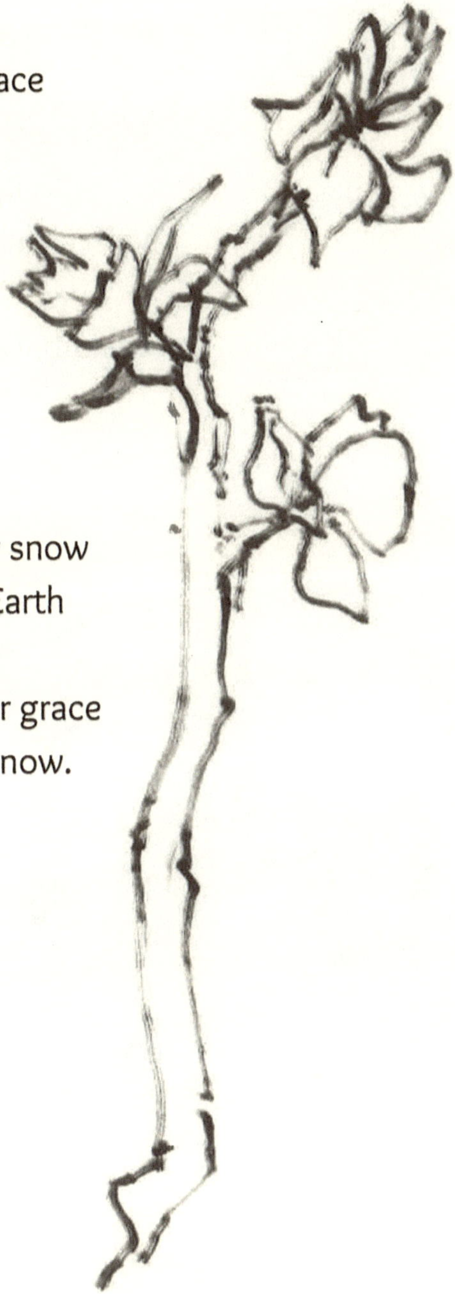

Today we have new snow
covering all Earth
in white love
of your grace
now.

Climate change
is upon us
with thanks for its blessings.
That's how
we initiate new interest
in living.

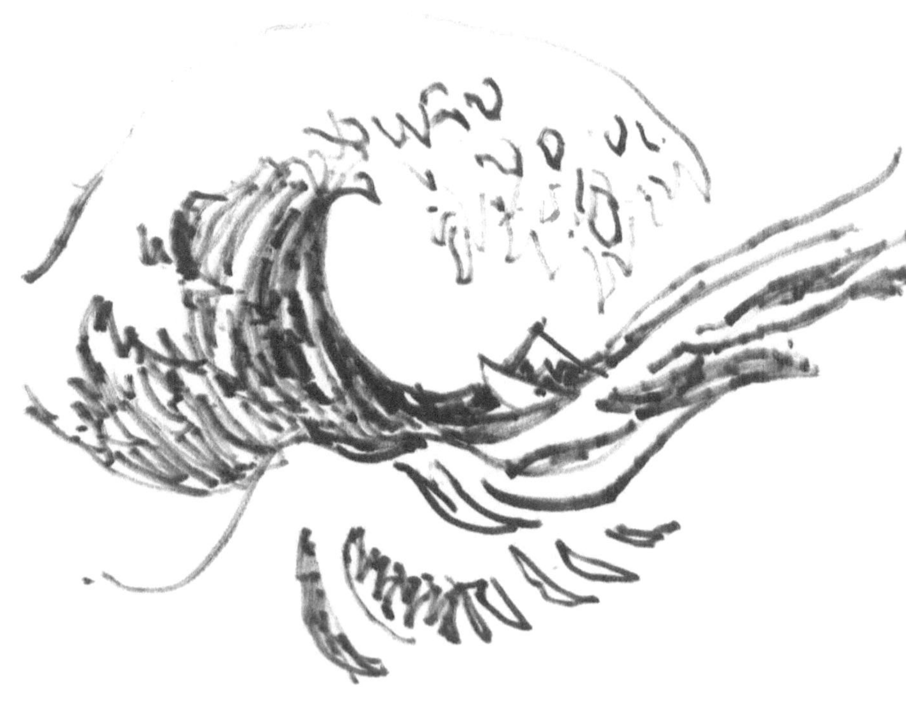

We are in love
>now
>with singing.
Life is a full song.
Its music completes
>our life
>>allows us
>to be free.

Freedom is a wing prayer.
We are
joy shows us
what we need
to do.
We are in love
with a moment of hope.

How can we behave
        with resilience of grace?
            cope
with these multiple choices
        of behavior
with absolute love.

        Rope in the delight!
Finger the touch of beauty,
        find deepest feelings
            scope.

The deep landscape
      of prayer, views of beyond,
            of happiness.
      We can hope
that each fragrance of earth
      flowers will repeat
      the abundance
            hope.

We will swallow the tastes
    and deep honey
    in honesty
    and truth.
        Grope
in all measures of swallowing
        delight.

Elope
with the marriage
of abundance,
of harmony.
Leap into faith.
Hope
is no burden: we can throw it away.
Instead, carry courage!

Soap
is cleanliness. Soap is clear.
Soap is every day honesty
to cope
with all differences,
make peace as a rule.
Gives us gratitude,
hope.

Now is the present
	when we know our way
to absolute truth:
		love.
It is the meaning of life.
It is the hearing
	the seeing
		above
all else. We become ourselves
	in service to God.
We are happier
	with love.

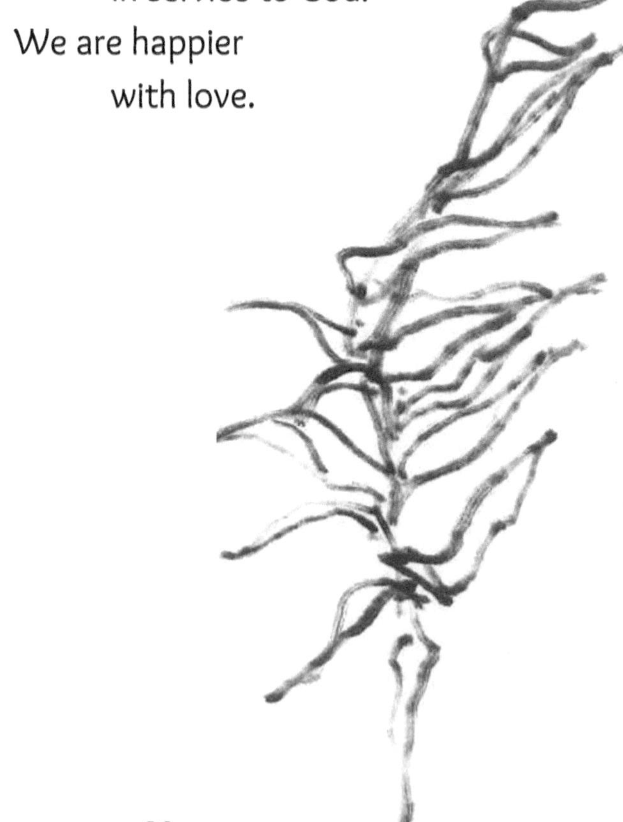

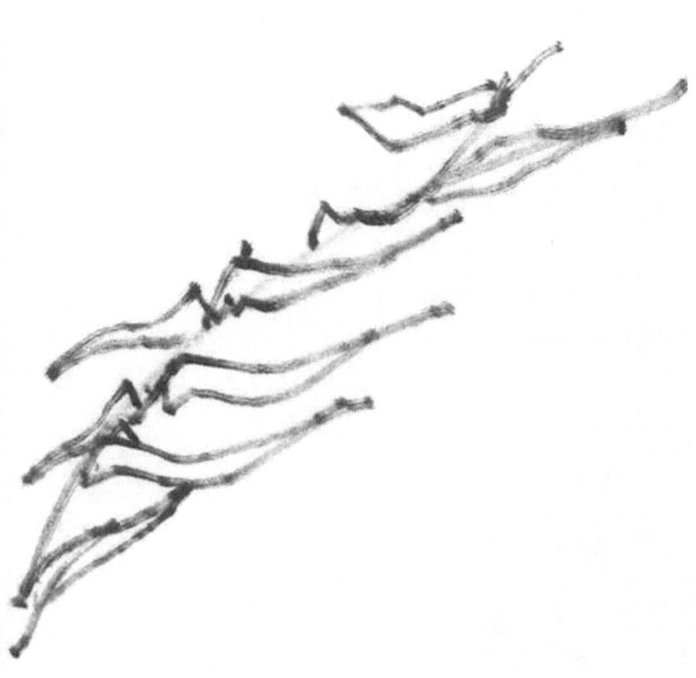

How are you going to speak now?
    With relish, with desire
        hopes above
        all else.
Now we are solvent.
Our honor is redeemed:
        reaching Spirit
            Dove.

We are alive with joy!
Our hearts know Heaven
in birdsong
a song's
move.

Onwards and upwards
we roam
filling our brains
with scents
colors, tastes,
love.

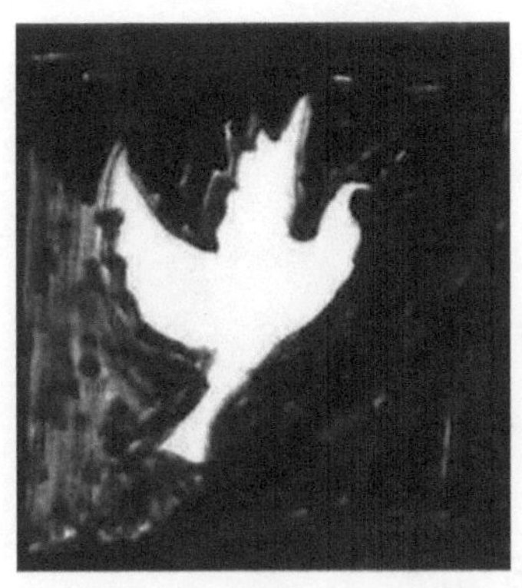

Where are the windmills
		to spin grain
to grind wheat into flour?
		Hover
	above us
We are the windmills ourselves
spinning God's spirit
		as love.

Are we windows into minds
of trees, of flowers,
     of Earth's treasures
          of fruit?
No. We are open heart's fragrance
     in windows of love seeking
          truth.
     Love's root.

We are flyers in high clouds
crying to the soul
wisdoms
new loot.

Now we are stepping stones
crossing the stream
of desire for God.

The fruit
of language is inherent
in soul.
All tongues of Spirit's
flames
are mute.

While we bask in darkness
        Sun is deep within
waiting to burst out
            in flames.

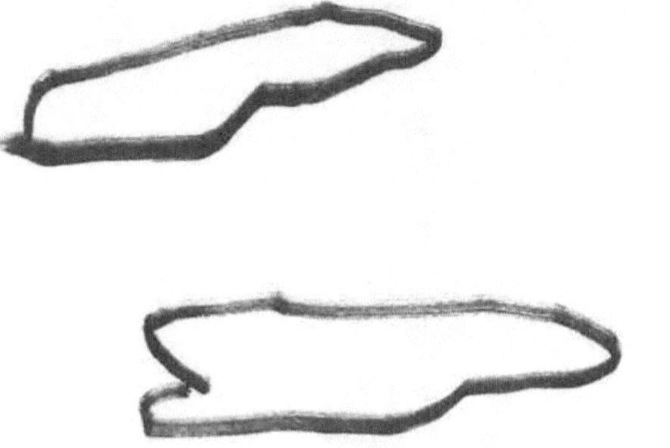

These flames are Spirit's claims
        of the Holy Ghost
        flying downward in a Dove's
            Name.

We, mankind, are one of these names.
We have spirit within us,
        the same
flooding all waters with Grace McKee
        as God.
All creatures of God
        share too.

Fame,
in the future as Heaven
is not enough
because Heaven
is tame!

Here in our arms, in our hearts,
in our breath, which is yours,
the same gift of smiling wonders
in all children of God
is miraculous!
Flame.

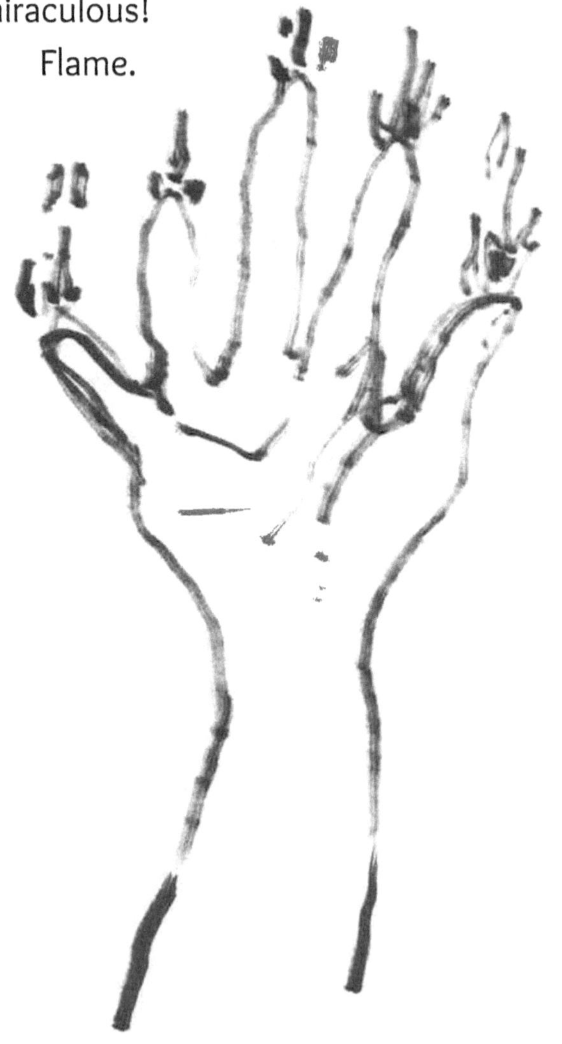

Where will we reside
        in this new Heaven?
In the here and now
        we frame
the horizons with harmony.
We set the world on fire,
        we are the torch,
                Flame.

To share the world with love
        now we are whole.
We are the movers,
            the same
fire-bearers, courageous
        and multitask
        workers towards peace:
            the frame
for marvels. We know what love is.

We name ourselves free. Free to observe.
The whole world is ours now.
We absorb
		shame.
We have opened our hearts
		to God's whisper.
It blooms in our minds
		like flame.
It is the flower of silence
		we greet
where Christ and Allah
		are same.

ADELE SERONDE

Adele Seronde's quiet *Canticles* of love offer reassurance of integrity and beauty in this time of global turbulence. They are written in a form of personal rather than Japanese haiku. We need simple, straight -forward expressions of our caring, and need to extend compassion and understanding to one another and to all living creatures.

Born in 1925, Seronde is a painter, poet and community activist. She has had solo and group exhibitions across America and in Italy. She has published or contributed to eight books of poetry, some used in our public schools. In the late 1960's, she served as a Co-Director for Visual Arts for "Summerthing," the Mayor of Boston's Neighborhood Arts Festival. In 1980, she founded Gardens for Humanity to help catalyze gardens in schools and urban areas, and wrote *Our Sacred Garden: the Living Earth.*

Currently finishing her new book, *Pegasus on Fire: Art, Nature and Spirit in Education*, Adele Seronde hopes you will enjoy this small tribute to the songs that live in all of our hearts.